E-CIGARETTE AND VAPING

RISKS

Other titles in the *Drug Risks* series include:

CONTENTS

The Rise of Vaping and E-Cigarettes

What Are E-Cigarettes?

E-cigarettes are battery-powered devices by which the liquid forms of various substances—such as nicotine, flavorings, and other chemicals—are heated into vapor and inhaled. The vapor takes the place of tobacco in traditional cigarettes and usually carries a higher concentration of nicotine.

Vaping has taken the world by storm. Anyone who doubts the popularity of e-cigarettes needs only to glance at these numbers: In 2011, 7 million people used e-cigarettes. By 2018, that number had reached 41 million. By 2021, the market research group Euromonitor predicts, there will be 55 million adults using e-cigarettes. E-cigarettes are particularly popular in the United States. In a July 2019 Gallup poll, 8 percent of adults reported vaping in the week before the poll, up from 4 percent in 2014.

Teens also are using e-cigarettes in astonishing numbers. The US Food and Drug Administration (FDA) reports that in 2019, over 5 million middle school and high school students were using e-cigarettes, and about 1 million of them used daily.

E-Cigarettes Are Harmful

The growing use of e-cigarettes and other electronic nicotine delivery systems (ENDS)—including vapes, vaporizers, vape pens, hookah pens, mods, and e-pipes—is troubling. E-cigarettes contain nicotine and other harmful chemicals. Experts say that e-cigarettes are addictive and cause health problems. Policy makers and parents alike find this especially worrying because so many young people are vaping regularly.

Many teens and other people who vape are unaware that e-cigarettes can adversely affect a user's lungs, heart, kidneys, and immune system. Thousands of e-cigarette users have ended up in emergency rooms with vaping injuries, some of which have been fatal. Seeing this, many teens have begun campaigning on social media and lobbying Congress to end the vaping epidemic plaguing their generation.

Some of these teens say they are tired of walking into a school restroom, hallway, or even classroom that is filled with e-cigarette aerosol. Teens who use vaping devices at school often report being able to do so undetected because ENDS devices are more discreet than cigarettes and their vapor is less offensive than cigarette smoke.

Experts say that e-cigarettes are addictive and cause health problems. Policy makers and parents alike find this especially worrying because so many young people are vaping regularly.

Like with the secondhand smoke from traditional cigarettes, the aerosol from e-cigarettes also can have negative consequences for others in the vicinity of the user. Dr. Stanton Glantz, director for the Center for Tobacco Control Research and Education at the University of California, San Francisco, explains, "If you are around somebody who is using e-cigarettes, you are breathing an aerosol of exhaled nicotine, ultra-fine particles, volatile organic compounds, and other toxins."[1]

Origin of E-Cigarettes

Awareness of health risks of e-cigarettes has only come about in the last few years. In part, this is because e-cigarettes are only a recent invention. While tobacco companies have been working to produce a nicotine aerosol generation device since 1963, Hon Lik patented and marketed the first e-cigarette four decades later.

Lik, a pharmacist from Shenyang in northeast China, was desperate to quit smoking cigarettes. He tried the traditional method of nicotine patches, as well as the methods lesser known to Western medicine, such as deer antler and ginseng, to quit his two-to-three-pack-a-day cigarette habit. He hoped to avoid the fate of his father, a smoker who died of lung cancer. One night, Lik had a nightmare that he was drowning in a sea before it suddenly turned into a cloud of vapor. Convinced that this had meaning, Lik detailed his nightmare on a notepad resting on a table next to his bed so that he would remember it in the morning. For him, his nightmare turned into a dream.

In 2003 Lik invented a device that simulated the sensation of smoking using vapor. The dream had inspired a patented invention that uses a high-frequency, piezoelectric ultrasound-emitting element to heat liquid into vapor. In 2004 the e-cigarette—a battery-operated device that heats liquid containing nicotine and turns it into vapor—was manufactured in Beijing, China. At first, manufacturers working twenty-four hours a day could not keep up with the high demand. Lik was proud of his invention. In an interview, he said, "My real passion, like many other inventors, is to leave some trace behind."[2] However, his device did not have the desired effect, which was to help him stop smoking tobacco cigarettes. *The Guardian* reports that he did not quit, but rather uses both.

E-cigarettes and vaping products are now widely available online and at millions of shops worldwide. Many users have turned to e-cigarettes in hopes of quitting their tobacco habit. Many others have no experience with traditional cigarettes. Both groups of users seem to be driving the industry's explosive growth. According to BIS Research (a global market intelligence, research, and advisory company), the e-cigarette and vaping industry's net worth was $20 billion in 2020 and projected to reach $46.9 billion by 2025.

Developments in Medical Research

With a larger population of users and the passing of time, medical experts are learning the health impacts of e-cigarettes. It is becoming increasingly clear that there are significant health consequences from vaping. In 2019, for example, a record number of people were hospitalized with lung injuries associated with e-cigarettes. The long-term health consequences of vaping are still largely unknown, however. Like with cigarettes in the 1900s, current e-cigarette users are essentially medical guinea pigs in a long-term study on the health implications of inhaling various toxicants over an extended period of time.

E-cigarettes seem to share a number of parallels with the tobacco industry. They have experienced growing popularity following their introduction to the market. Use is associated with many cases of sickness and death. And there are secondhand effects for nonusers. It also seems likely that, over time, the known health consequences of vaping will be a deterrent.

CHAPTER ONE

A Pervasive Problem

Chance Ammirata vaped for the first time when he was a junior in a Florida high school. He was hooked on e-cigarettes after three hits. In a 2019 interview, he said, "I felt this buzz and it was like all of the anxiety and stress that I had [went away]. . . . From that point on, every single day that I tried going without it felt like too much for me."[3]

Ammirata had been vaping for about a year and a half when he began to experience serious health problems. The problems began with pain on his side, similar to the sensation of a pulled muscle. The discomfort quickly grew worse. Ammirata recalls, "I remember [my friend] made me laugh and it felt like my chest was collapsing, like I was having a heart attack."[4] He was hospitalized with a collapsed lung. Surgeons had to insert a tube into his lung to keep it inflated. They subsequently did an emergency surgery to repair the hole that caused the collapse. Doctors also discovered that Ammirata's lungs were covered in black dots, a sign that his lungs were injured from infection or inflammation. The doctors told Ammirata his lungs could take years to heal. The condition affects his ability to do the things he enjoys such as jogging, scuba diving, and traveling.

Rising Use

Ammirata's experience is not unique. Lung injuries across the country have made headlines as the use of e-cigarettes increases over time. Many of vaping's casualties are young. People under thirty are the largest consumer group of e-cigarettes. A 2019 Pew Research Center report shows that vaping is most widespread among young adults. The Pew survey showed that 20 percent of Americans ages eighteen to twenty-nine vape compared with 8 percent of Americans ages thirty to sixty-four. The same survey showed that only 1 percent of Americans sixty-five and older vape.

Other surveys have revealed widespread e-cigarette use among teens. The percentage of middle school and high school students who use e-cigarettes is not only high: it is increasing. Truth Initiative, a nonprofit public health organization, reports that the rate of use by middle schoolers rose from 0.6 percent in 2011 to 10.5 percent in 2019. High school students' use also has increased in recent years. In 2017, 11 percent of high school students reported using an e-cigarette in the thirty days before the survey. By 2019, that number had jumped to 27.5 percent. The recent political and media attention to the dangers of vaping is partly due to statistics that show the continuing rise in teen use. In December 2018, the US Surgeon General Vice Admiral Jerome M. Adams warned, "E-cigarette use among youth has skyrocketed in the past year at a rate of epidemic proportions."[5]

Many analysts believe that young people are using because they are enticed by the flavors and because their friends are vaping. In a 2019 National Youth Tobacco Survey—an annual, school-based, self-administered survey of US students in grades six through twelve—30 percent of the respondents said that they use e-cigarettes because friends or family use them. Meanwhile, 35 percent of those surveyed acknowledge that they vape because of the flavors of the pods. There are dessert varieties, like apple pie, cannoli, and cotton candy. Fruit choices such as blueberry, peach, coconut,

"I felt this buzz and it was like all of the anxiety and stress that I had [went away]. . . . From that point on, every single day that I tried going without it felt like too much for me."[3]

—Chance Ammirata, former vaper

"E-cigarette use among youth has skyrocketed in the past year at a rate of epidemic proportions."[5]

—Vice Admiral Jerome M. Adams, US surgeon general

Teen E-Cigarette Use Increases

E-cigarette use among eighth, tenth, and twelfth grade students increased significantly between 2017 and 2019, according to an annual survey conducted by the University of Michigan. Despite national public health campaigns warning of the dangers, researchers found that teen vaping more than doubled in all three grades during this three-year period.

Teen Vaping, 2017–2019

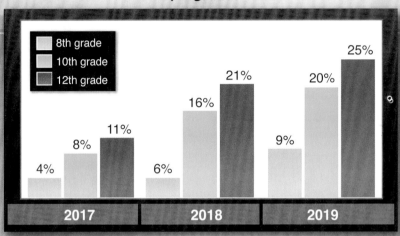

Source: Sheila Kaplan, "Teen Vaping Rises Sharply Again this Year," *New York Times*, September 18, 2019. www.nytimes.com.

and strawberry also fill the shelves of vape shops. Teens surveyed said that they prefer mango and mint in particular.

Analysts also point to e-cigarette companies' advertising campaigns as influencing the rise in teen use. Company executives claim that their product's purpose is to provide a healthier alternative to smoking. E-cigarettes, they say, are meant to be a smoking cessation aid, not an introduction to nicotine. But critics argue that their advertising campaign on social media suggests otherwise. Companies like JUUL, which has the largest share of the e-cigarette market, have hired brand influencers to use their product and post impressions on Instagram. Many concerned parents and policy makers contend that brand influencers on social media appeal to young people rather than to people who are trying to quit smoking cigarettes.

Contrary to the inventor Hon Lik's dream of the e-cigarette becoming a method with which to quit smoking, experts are concerned that vaping is a gateway for teens in particular to use other tobacco products in the future. For young adults, vaping does not seem to be about quitting smoking. Michael Blaha, a professor of medicine at Johns Hopkins, directs clinical research at the Ciccarone Center for the Prevention of Cardiovascular Disease. He explains, "Our own literature suggests that 2 million young adults use electronic cigarettes as their first nicotine-based product. They're not trying to quit smoking—they've never smoked before."[6] Only 10 percent of respondents in the 2019 National Youth Tobacco Survey said that they vape to cut down on other tobacco products.

Vaping Marijuana

Many people believe that vaping marijuana is safer than smoking it. Recent evidence suggests that might not be the case. A 2018 study revealed that people who vaped marijuana had higher concentrations of THC, the psychoactive chemical in marijuana, in their bloodstream than did those who smoked it. Short-term effects of THC include hallucinations, delusions, psychosis, impaired memory, difficulty problem solving and thinking, altered sense of time, mood swings, impaired body movement, and altered senses. Research is still determining the long-term effects of THC.

In addition to the intensified side effects from THC, vaping exposes the lungs to other chemicals from the pods that smoking marijuana the traditional way or ingesting it does not. By November 2019, 2,290 cases of lung disease linked to vaping were reported across the United States, and at least forty-seven people had died. Most of those people reported using vaping products that contained THC. Some medical experts believe that vitamin E acetate, an oil derived from the vitamin to dilute THC, is causing the problem. As a result of the rise in lung injuries, the CDC has issued a recommendation that people avoid vaping products that contain THC.

Vaping as a Way to Quit Smoking Cigarettes

The popularity of e-cigarettes has grown, even if only in small part, because some people use it as a way to stop smoking. JUUL peppers its website with several testimonials. The website states, "The community of over one million adult smokers who have switched are at the heart of our mission."[7] JUUL has convinced many former smokers to trade in their pack of cigarettes for an e-cigarette. Older adults are more likely than younger people to begin vaping to stop using other tobacco products. As it turns out, though, e-cigarettes might not even be the most useful cessation aid. High hopes are often dashed with the return to smoking traditional cigarettes and concerns that e-cigarettes have significant health consequences.

JUUL has convinced many former smokers to swap cigarettes for e-cigarettes. Older adults are more likely than younger people to begin vaping in order to stop using other tobacco products.

This was true for Nick English. He was a casual smoker but had issues with coughing and phlegm afterwards. He first considered substituting traditional cigarettes with vaping after he saw a JUUL ad promoting its e-cigarettes as a smoking cessation aid. English bought an e-cigarette and settled on the crème brûlée flavor pod. He never believed e-cigarettes were harmless, just less harmful than traditional cigarettes. He liked that the flavor pods did not make his breath stink and that he could vape inside in more places than he could smoke. Although he only smoked two or three cigarettes a day before vaping, he became much more dependent on the e-cigarette and felt its consequences. In a 2018 magazine article, English writes, "Eventually, I was vaping pretty much all day, every day. My lung capacity was absolutely destroyed. I couldn't do cardio to save my life; walking up stairs sucked the wind out of me."[8] Finding that vaping was just too easy, English went back to smoking traditional cigarettes.

"Eventually, I was vaping pretty much all day, every day. My lung capacity was absolutely destroyed. I couldn't do cardio to save my life; walking up stairs sucked the wind out of me."[8]

—Nick English, user of e-cigarettes for nicotine replacement

Research Has Mixed Results

Some research findings are consistent with English's story, while others show some benefit to using e-cigarettes for quitting the use of traditional cigarettes. A 2019 study published in *JAMA Internal Medicine* concludes that e-cigarettes are useful in helping people stop smoking initially. But the study also found that their use as a cessation aid was associated with an increased rate of smoking relapse after two years. On the other hand, a study published in a 2019 article of the *New England Journal of Medicine* concludes that "e-cigarettes were more effective for smoking cessation than nicotine-replacement therapy, when both products were accompanied by behavioral support."[9]

Despite these findings, many medical experts argue that there are less harmful and more effective ways to quit a smoking habit.

There is general agreement among medical experts that smokers should not go back to smoking traditional cigarettes to stop vaping.

Based on an interview with Dr. Norman Edelman, Senior Scientific Advisor for the American Lung Association, English writes that "the most effective methods involve some sort of pharmaceutical, either nicotine replacement patches or pills, combined with a program that helps you deal with the problems of quitting smoking."[10]

There is general agreement among medical experts that a smoker should not go back to smoking traditional cigarettes to stop vaping. There is not agreement, however, that a person who uses traditional cigarettes should use e-cigarettes as a cessation aid. As of mid-2020, the FDA had not yet approved them as such. Dr. Robert Shmerling, faculty editor of Harvard Health Publishing, argues, "Vaping could soon get approval from the FDA as a smoking cessation aid, but even if that happens, it should not be the first choice given how much is still unknown."[11]

Nicotine and Other Harmful Chemicals

The continuing rise in vaping is a significant problem because e-cigarettes contain nicotine and other harmful chemicals. Nicotine is an addictive drug. Chance Ammirata, for example, reported that he was addicted to e-cigarettes after only three hits. There are also debates over the long-term effects of nicotine in e-cigarettes. It raises the heart rate and blood pressure in the user. While e-cigarette users say they notice an increased focus and energy, nicotine dulls the senses in the long term. Despite its addictive quality and health consequences, many users report that they were unaware that e-cigarettes contained nicotine. According to data from the Centers for Disease Control and Prevention (CDC), in 2018, 63 percent of users were unaware that JUUL pods contain nicotine.

Nicotine is not the only health concern arising from e-cigarette use. The aerosol for e-cigarettes contains harmful chemicals. Little was known about the aerosol when the e-cigarette came on the US market in 2006. At that time, it was not unusual to see people vaping in shopping malls, restaurants, and other indoor public places. There was a common misconception that the vapor in the air coming from e-cigarettes was simply water. But it is not.

E-cigarettes use batteries to heat chemicals like propylene glycol or vegetable glycerin. Some of these chemicals are even more harmful when they are heated. For example, propylene glycol turns into propylene oxide, a carcinogen. Additionally, diacetyl is used to flavor an estimated 75 percent of the pods. The inhalation of diacetyl leads to popcorn lung, a condition that damages the lungs' airways, making a person cough and feel out of breath. The heated liquid can also produce unintended dangerous byproducts when inhaled—including heavy metals such as lead, tin, aluminum, and nickel. Medical experts warn in a 2019 American Academy of Pediatrics journal article, "While [e-cigarettes] have been marketed as producing a 'harmless water vapor', do not be fooled. The heating of the compounds in the liquid creates particulates, volatile organic compounds, and tobacco-specific nitrosamines, among other toxic chemicals, all of which can provoke inflammatory reactions in the lungs and circulation."[12]

Health Complications

According to the CDC, these inflammatory reactions and acute respiratory problems in e-cigarette users have led to thousands of hospitalizations across the United States.

Among them was nineteen-year-old Cara Fraser. After a year of vaping e-cigarettes, Fraser could not breathe on her own. Doctors put her into a medically induced coma for a week and warned her family that she might not survive. She was fortunate; she did recover. She decided to post her story on social media to encourage other users to quit vaping. In an interview, Fraser

Big Tobacco's Relationship with E-Cigarettes

Declining sales of traditional cigarettes have cost tobacco companies money, but they have recouped some of their losses by getting into the e-cigarette market. Imperial Brands, manufacturer of Salem and Kool cigarettes, sells the Blu e-cigarette brand. British American Tobacco, maker of Newport and Camel brands, sells Vuse. Altria, which owns the Marlboro name, owns a one-third stake in JUUL.

Decades of denial by tobacco companies about the connection between smoking and lung cancer lead some people to wonder if something similar could happen with e-cigarettes. In a 2019 opinion piece, Brendon Stiles, a cardiothoracic surgeon, and Steve Alperin, the CEO of SurvivorNet, a media outlet for cancer information, write, "We remain shockingly ignorant about what the combustible liquids within e-cigarettes actually contain. We already made that mistake with tobacco and cigarettes. . . . Let's not repeat those mistakes and regrets with e-cigarettes and vaping."

Brendon Stiles and Steve Alperin, "We Ignored the Evidence Linking Cigarettes to Cancer. Let's Not Do That with Vaping," *The Guardian*, February 16, 2019. www.theguardian.com.

explains why she posted her story. She said, "I just really wanted to help one person. Not only was it hard physically it was very hard mentally to go through that. I didn't want anyone else to go through it."[13]

Despite the large number of hospitalizations from lung injuries, many people still do not know the dangers of vaping. Older people are more likely than younger people to believe that vaping is harmful to a person's health. In a July 2018 Gallup survey, 22 percent of respondents under thirty years old believed that vaping is very harmful to one's health. In comparison, 40 percent of respondents ages thirty to sixty-four and 48 percent of those sixty-five and older thought vaping is very harmful. Meanwhile, over 80 percent of the respondents in all three age categories agree that smoking conventional cigarettes is very harmful. The age variations in the perceptions of danger associated with vaping help to explain why vaping is more popular among younger adults.

Overall e-cigarette use is growing, particularly among teens in the United States. This is problematic because e-cigarettes contain nicotine and other harmful chemicals. Many users are unaware of the presence of these chemicals or what the health consequences of inhaling them might be.

CHAPTER TWO

Consequences of Vaping

Vaping can kill. The CDC reports that between June 2019 and February 2020, there were sixty-eight deaths from lung injuries associated with e-cigarettes and vaping. The people who died lived in states all across the country, and their ages range from fifteen to seventy-five. Denis Byrne Jr. was among them. He was seventeen years old and had recently graduated from Salesian High School in New Rochelle, New York. On October 4, 2019, Byrne died from a lung injury associated with e-cigarette use. The chief medical examiner, Dr. Barbara Sampson, identified vaping as the cause of the young man's death. She said, "Following a thorough medical investigation by the Office of Chief Medical Examiner, we have determined that the decedent died from complications from the usage of electronic vaping products."[14]

> "We are seeing that severe lung damage, and even death, can occur with just short-term use of these products."[15]
>
> —Dr. Philip Huang, Dallas County health director

Until that point in time, Byrne was recorded as the youngest person to die from EVALI (e-cigarette- or vaping-associated lung injury), the official name for vaping injuries. That changed just two months later when a fifteen-year-old from Texas died from vaping injuries. Dr. Philip Huang, the Dallas County health director, did not identify the teen but said in a statement that EVALI injuries sometimes occur in new users. One hospitalized teen, he noted, had only been vaping for a month. Huang states, "We are seeing that severe lung damage, and even death, can occur with just short-term use of these products."[15]

Acute Illness from Vaping

Not everyone who develops EVALI dies; many have been hospitalized and recovered (although not always fully). In February 2020, the CDC said that 2,807 cases had been reported from all US states, the District of Columbia, Puerto Rico, and the US Virgin Islands. The average age of the patients was twenty-four years old, but some were as young as thirteen and as old as eighty-five. September 2019 had the highest number of EVALI hospitalization cases.

Daniel Ament, a seventeen-year-old high school junior from Grosse Pointe, Michigan, was among them. He was an avid

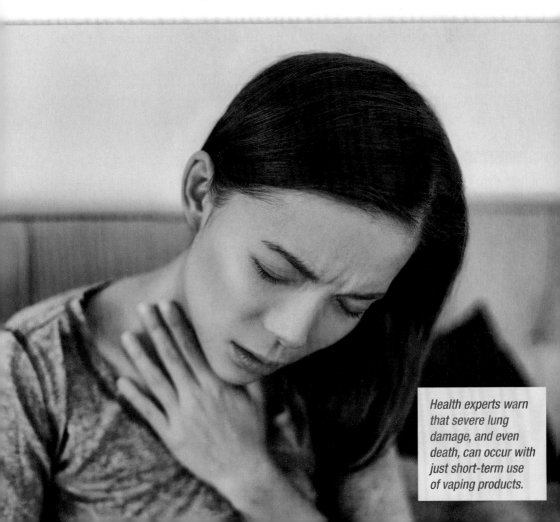

Health experts warn that severe lung damage, and even death, can occur with just short-term use of vaping products.

runner and sailor before vaping damaged his lungs. Ament told an interviewer that he first tried vaping in December 2018. In the summer of 2019, Ament began sharing e-cigarettes with his friends at parties, and then vaping became a daily habit. He intended to quit when school started again. By early September 2019, however, he began to feel ill. At first, he experienced headaches, but his health quickly deteriorated from there. It was increasingly clear that his lungs were compromised when he began experiencing pneumonia-like symptoms such as cough, shortness of breath, and chest pains. Ament was put on life support for twenty-nine days and given only a 10 percent chance of survival. In October 2019, the doctors made a decision to give him a double lung transplant. Dr. Hassan Nemeh, a thoracic surgeon, stated, "We had to transplant him or pull support. I truly don't think he had a lot of time left." Nemeh further recounted that Ament's lungs were "like truck rubber" and "so scarred they didn't even deflate."[16]

Ament survived his injury, but not without consequences. He lost forty pounds and continues to take twenty medications per day associated with the transplant. While in public, he has to wear a mask to protect his lungs from infection. Ament earlier had dreams of attending military college, but he can no longer complete the physical requirements to do so. Instead he has created the nonprofit Fight4Wellness to educate other young people about the risks of vaping. He admits that when the doctors first told him that his lung injury was from vaping, he had a hard time believing it. In a news interview he says, "It just didn't make sense because why didn't it happen to other people that had been vaping for years? Why didn't it happen to someone else close to me that, I was hitting their stuff, so how did the chemicals affect me, not them?"[17]

"It just didn't make sense because why didn't it happen to other people that had been vaping for years? Why didn't it happen to someone else close to me that, I was hitting their stuff, so how did the chemicals affect me, not them?"[17]

—Daniel Ament, seventeen, survivor of EVALI and a related double lung transplant

Exploding E-Cigarettes and Vape Pens

The mysterious lung disease that has claimed dozens of lives is not the only known hazard of vaping. In 2017, the federal government reported 195 instances in which an e-cigarette exploded or caught fire. Usually, the devices exploded while in use or while being stored in a pocket. The FDA has stated that it is not certain why some devices explode, but battery-related issues might be the cause. Of the explosions, 133 led to injuries, and thirty-eight of them were severe. These statistics were compiled by the Federal Emergency Management Agency's (FEMA) US Fire Administration for the period between 2009 and 2016. The report concludes that while such explosions are uncommon, they are dangerous and often life-altering when they happen.

In one case in particular, a vape pen explosion was life-ending. On May 5, 2018, firefighters found the body of thirty-eight-year-old Tallmadge D'Elia inside his burning home in St. Petersburg, Florida. An autopsy found that an explosion sent two pieces of a vape pen into D'Elia's cranium. The autopsy report ruled his cause of death to be "projectile wound of the head," but he also had burns on 80 percent of his body.

Quoted in CBS and AP, "Shrapnel from Exploding Vape Pen Kills Florida Man, Autopsy Report Says," CBS News, May 16, 2018. www.cbsnews.com.

EVALI and Aerosol Additives

Ament was not the only one asking that question. Members of the public and medical professionals alike were puzzled by lung illnesses that had sent so many vapers to the hospital. Direct correlations are still somewhat of a mystery, but the culprits are believed to be devices that have been altered and the use of vitamin E acetate as an additive. Dr. Michael Blaha, a professor at Johns Hopkins School of Medicine and Epidemiology, explains, "[EVALI] cases appear to predominantly affect people who modify their vaping devices or use black market modified e-liquids.

This is especially true for vaping products containing tetrahydro-cannabinol (THC)."[18]

The CDC says that roughly 80 percent of EVALI cases had reported using vaping products that contained THC, the active ingredient in marijuana. Many of the THC-containing e-cigarettes or vaping products use vitamin E acetate as an additive. Although vitamin E acetate is not problematic when ingested in food or as a dietary supplement, the CDC states, "research suggests that when vitamin E acetate is inhaled, it may interfere with normal lung functioning."[19] In addition, a third of the people who reported vaping only nicotine reported that they used vaping devices from informal (rather than commercial) sources. Informal sources are more likely to contain additives, which sellers use to make their more expensive ingredients last longer. Vitamin E acetate and other additives in vaping aerosol are particularly dangerous when inhaled.

Cases of people being hospitalized with EVALI decreased after the peak in September 2019. The CDC suspects that a reduction in cases nationwide was due to growing public awareness of the dangers of vaping THC, the removal of vitamin E acetate from some vaping products, and law enforcement interventions in the use of illicit vaping products. Despite the reduction in EVALI hospitalizations since September 2019, it is clear that e-cigarettes and vaping are far from harmless.

Popcorn Lung

Vaping can cause both EVALI and popcorn lung, the nickname for bronchiolitis obliterans. In EVALI cases, patients have damage to their alveoli, the small air sacs in their lungs. But when people have popcorn lung, the smallest airways in the lungs are inflamed and obstructed. Popcorn lung is a rare lung disease that was named in 2000, when eight workers at a microwave popcorn factory in Missouri were afflicted from accidentally inhaling vaporized diacetyl. The chemical diacetyl is used to give popcorn the buttery flavor. It is also used as a flavoring agent in e-cigarettes. When ingested, diacetyl is not a problem for the lungs. When

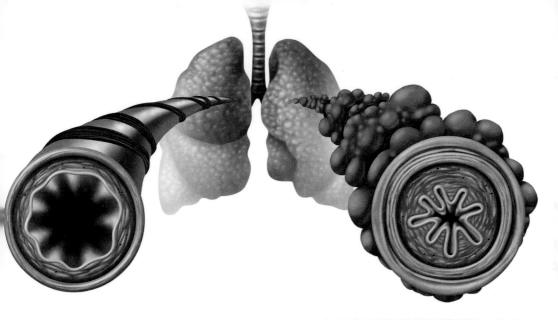

the popcorn workers and e-cigarette users inhale it, however, it can lead to bronchiolitis.

In the case of a seventeen-year-old in Canada, vaping was likely the cause of popcorn lung. The teen, who worked in a fast-food restaurant, reported that he vaped daily for the five months preceding the development of symptoms. He used the flavors "dew mountain," "green apple," and "cotton candy," which he bought online. Sometimes, he said, he added THC to his vaping fluid. In 2019, he went to the emergency room because he had difficulty breathing, severe cough, fever, and nausea. His symptoms worsened, and he was admitted to the intensive care unit. There, he was placed on an extracorporeal membrane oxygenation (ECMO) machine, which circulates blood through an artificial lung outside the body. Imaging tests confirmed that the teen had popcorn lung. Doctors referred him to a lung transplant center, but he did not require a transplant in the end. Still, he spent nearly fifty days in the hospital. In November 2019, LiveScience reports, "It appears that he now has chronic damage to his airways and his exercise ability is limited. . . . The teen isn't using e-cigarettes, marijuana or tobacco products anymore."[20]

The connection between diacetyl and bronchiolitis obliterans was established in 2000 with the popcorn factory workers in Missouri. This likely played a role in prompting the American Lung Association's subsequent warning about the health effects of inhaling diacetyl with e-cigarette use. In July 2016 the association called on the FDA to ban the use of diacetyl and other harmful chemicals in e-cigarettes. And an article published in the *Canadian Medical Association Journal* in December 2019 called for more research into the health risks posed by e-cigarettes. "This case of severe acute bronchiolitis . . . in a previously healthy Canadian youth, may represent vaping-associated bronchiolitis obliterans . . . underscoring the need for further research into all potentially toxic components of e-liquids and tighter regulation of e-cigarettes."[21]

EVALI and popcorn lung are two conditions that afflict the lungs of e-cigarette users, but there are likely more. For example, e-cigarette users have often reported shortness of breath and coughing. It is unknown, however, if certain preexisting conditions—asthma for example—make people more prone to lung disease from e-cigarettes. Many other unknowns exist, which makes a full understanding of vaping-related illnesses challenging. Dr. Robert Shmerling describes some of the questions that still need answers. In September 2019, he wrote, "Is [lung disease] more common among younger individuals? Does use of e-cigarettes cause the lung disease? Or is an added substance (such as marijuana) or another contaminant the culprit? Since the FDA's regulation of e-cigarettes is still evolving, it's particularly difficult to get answers."[22]

Compromised Immune System

Vaping can also suppress the immune system, making e-cigarette users more susceptible to illnesses and infections, and possibly increases the likelihood of pneumonia. A 2018 study published in the journal *Thorax* reveals that in laboratory studies on lung tissue, the vapor from e-cigarettes disabled vital immune cells and increased inflammation. This experiment is consistent with a 2015 Johns Hopkins University study on mice, which concluded that exposure to e-cigarette vapor limited the mice's immune system and their ability to fight viral and bacterial infections in the lungs. A study in 2019 published in the *Journal of Clinical Investigation* further concludes, "Immune cells isolated from the lungs of mice exposed to chronic vape (ENDS), but not air or smoke, show large abnormal translucent bodies inside the cells [that] are full of fat."[23] The overwhelming amounts of fat affected their ability to fight against pathogens.

Consistent with these findings, many people who vape have claimed to feel chronically ill. These studies suggest vaping potentially is a contributing factor. For example, Simah Herman's immune system might have been compromised from vaping. She

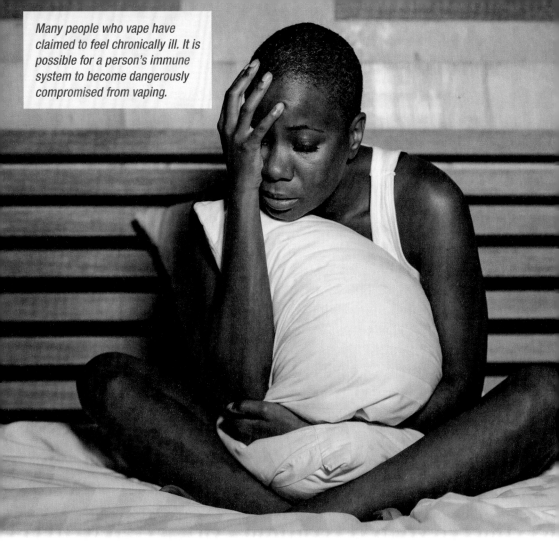

Many people who vape have claimed to feel chronically ill. It is possible for a person's immune system to become dangerously compromised from vaping.

began using e-cigarettes when she was fifteen. During the two years that she vaped, Herman told an interviewer in 2019, she felt sick all the time and lost fifty pounds "without trying." She also reported frequently feeling dizzy and nauseous and missing school often. It is possible that Herman felt chronically ill as a result of disabled immune cells. In August 2019, illness almost turned to tragedy. Herman's father rushed her to the hospital because she could not breathe. The doctors put her on a ventilator and induced a coma. A chest X-ray revealed that her lungs were inflamed and full of fluid. Five days later, Herman woke from her coma, asked for a pen because she could not speak and wrote a sign that read, "I want to start a no vaping campaign."[24]

Vaping and the Heart

E-cigarettes and vaping are also harmful to the vascular system. Microscopic particles in the aerosol are linked to high blood pressure, coronary artery disease, and heart attacks. The vapor causes damage to the endothelial cells, which line the interior of blood vessels, lymphatic vessels, and the heart. A November 2019 article in the *European Heart Journal* finds that e-cigarette vapor compromises the vascular system even in people who regularly smoke traditional cigarettes. They identified e-cigarette vapor's toxic aldehyde acrolein (an herbicide most often used to kill weeds) as the culprit for heart damage. The study states, "We found that a single episode of e-cigarette smoking induced endothelial dysfunction even in chronic smokers."[25]

Stephen Davies, a forty-nine-year-old with four children, blames e-cigarettes for his heart attack and cardiac arrest in 2019. Davies smoked traditional cigarettes for twenty years before he switched to vaping in 2014, believing that it was the healthier alternative. Five years later, on April 5, 2019, he experienced shortness of breath and jaw pain at work. Later that evening, he had indigestion, took some medication, and went to bed. In the middle of the night, he woke up in a tremendous amount of pain and unable to breathe. His wife called the paramedics. Davies was having a heart attack. When his heart stopped on the way to the hospital, paramedics worked to restart it. When he arrived at the hospital, a cardiac surgeon placed a stent in his heart. After two days in the hospital, Davies was stable. In the discharge notes, his cardiologist, Dr. Oliver Gosling, wrote, "Transthoracic echo showed level of heart failure of 40% with extensive wall motion abnormalities. Mr. Davies . . . was discharged home after being advised to stop vaping and referred for cardiac rehabilitation."[26]

Davies followed the doctor's advice and stopped vaping. Despite his many years of smoking (before switching to vaping), in a December 2019 interview he said, "Before my heart attack, I've always been healthy—I stayed fit, my cholesterol was really low,

I maintained a healthy weight. The doctors couldn't 100 per cent guarantee it was because I was vaping, but my wife and I swear it was the vape pen that did this to me."[27]

Questions About Long-Term Effects

Medical research on the health risks of vaping is still relatively new. That might explain why so many people believe that e-cigarettes are a healthy alternative to traditional cigarettes. This is also the message coming from e-cigarette makers, who have promoted their vaping products as safer than cigarettes made from tobacco. From a scientific perspective, however, there remain many unknowns. Researchers are looking into the effects of e-cigarettes on the heart, lungs, and other body organs. They are also investigating possible links between the chemicals used in the aerosol of e-cigarettes and cancer.

Some experts recall how many years passed before medical researchers, health professionals, and the public acknowledged and understood the health hazards of smoking. In the 1930s, almost no one considered cigarettes to be a cause of lung cancer. In 1939 Dr. Evarts Graham, a pioneer of lung cancer surgery, mocked the idea that there was a connection between the two. He argued, "Yes, there is a parallel between the sale of cigarettes and the incidence of cancer of the lung, but there is also a parallel between the sale of nylon stockings and the incidence of lung cancer."[28] Today, though, the connection between smoking traditional cigarettes and lung cancer is irrefutable.

> "The doctors couldn't 100 per cent guarantee [the heart attack] was because I was vaping, but my wife and I swear it was the vape pen that did this to me."[27]
>
> —Stephen Davies, heart attack and cardiac arrest survivor

Stiles and Alperin argue that it is important to not let years pass once again without determining for certain the risks of vaping. They write, "There are few things as heartbreaking as seeing the regret and self-blame of a former smoker newly diagnosed with lung cancer long after he or she got wise and gave up their cigarettes.

Let's not repeat those mistakes and regrets with e-cigarettes and vaping."[29]

Many experts believe there will be long-term connections between vaping and a variety of afflictions. Dr. Brandon T. Larsen, a surgical pathologist at the Mayo Clinic in Scottsdale, Arizona, said, "Based on the severity of injury we see, at least in some of these cases, I wouldn't be surprised if we wind up with people down the road having chronic respiratory problems from this. Some seem to recover. I don't think we know what the long-term consequences will be."[30]

"I don't think we know what the long-term consequences will be."[30]

—Dr. Brandon T. Larsen, surgical pathologist at the Mayo Clinic

CHAPTER THREE

Addicted to Vaping

Kari Paul, twenty-five, had a tough time quitting her vaping habit. Like many others, Paul found e-cigarettes more appealing than traditional cigarettes. For one thing, they did not stink. Plus, Paul felt there was even a glamor about them because fashion models like Gigi Hadid were vaping. Prior to buying a JUUL starter kit in September 2018, she was a casual cigarette smoker—having one every now and then when she was at a bar or out with friends. Less than a year after her e-cigarette purchase, she was completely dependent on it. She writes, "I was often Juuling in my pajamas the last thing before bed and the first thing when I woke up. I Juuled on bike rides, on plane bathrooms, and at the office. Once I repeatedly hit my Juul on a kayak as I floated through the rivers of northern California, storing the device in my swimsuit top."[31]

When reports of lung injuries from vaping began to surface, Paul made the decision to quit. She describes the seventy-two hours following her last hit on JUUL to be "hellish" and "the worst hours of her life." She writes, "I biked manically, I cried publicly, I grew irritated at nearly every sound I heard."[32] In the end, though, she was successful in quitting.

Nicotine and the Brain

Paul was able to quit vaping on her first attempt, but many people try quitting multiple times and still do not succeed. In June 2019, Truth Initiative reports that after thirty days of using the vaping support line to quit, only 15 percent of the participants were abstaining. Experts say that vaping is more addictive than smoking. Whether consumers buy a vaping device to put an end to their pack-a-day habit or as their introduction to nicotine, they find that once they start, it is extraordinarily difficult to stop. Judith Grisel, neuroscientist and author of *Never Enough: The Neuroscience and Experience of Addiction*, explains why vaping is even more addictive than smoking: "The delivery of nicotine in vapes is even quicker than cigarettes, which is hard to do. That's the biggest factor in addictive liability if it's the same chemical: the speed with which you get the hit."[33] There are many things that make e-cigarettes so addictive.

As with cigarettes, people vape for the nicotine. Nicotine is among the most common addictions in the United States. According to Addiction Center—an organization that works with

"I was often Juuling in my pajamas the last thing before bed and the first thing when I woke up. I Juuled on bike rides, on plane bathrooms, and at the office."[31]

—Kari Paul, former e-cigarette addict

Whether consumers buy a vaping device to put an end to their pack-a-day habit or as their introduction to nicotine, they find that once they start, it is extraordinarily difficult to stop.

treatment facilities to provide treatment counseling, rehab placement, and financial consultations to addicts—there are 40–60 million Americans addicted to nicotine. Addiction Center further reports that two-thirds of Americans who have tried products with nicotine subsequently become dependent on them at some point in their lives. Smoking and vaping are both hard to stop doing because nicotine is highly addictive. Nicotine makes users feel relaxed when they are stressed. It also increases alertness and the ability to concentrate. According to Judith Grisel, a former smoker herself, "[Nicotine is] almost a guaranteed addiction. Some people can drink alcohol without developing a problem, not everyone who takes opiates recreationally has a problem, but pretty much everyone likes the feeling of nicotine."[34] In fact, the CDC reports, nicotine is so captivating and soothing that 14 percent of American adults continued smoking in 2018 despite common knowledge of the link between cigarette smoking and death.

Nicotine causes addiction by hijacking the reward center of the brain. Specifically, it stimulates the release of dopamine. Dopamine causes euphoria and calmness and is what makes people feel good. While its release is naturally stimulated by activities like exercising and listening to music, it is released in greater amounts with the use of nicotine and other drugs. Vapers chase that feel-good feeling from the brain's dopamine release when they inhale the aerosol containing nicotine in their e-cigarette. When the dopamine levels go back down, users are left feeling tired and lacking energy. At that point, vapers reach for their e-cigarette to get that euphoric feeling again. The National Institute on Drug Abuse explains, "[T]his dopamine signal 'teaches' the brain to repeat the behavior of taking the drug. Smokers' brains have *learned* to smoke, and just like unlearning to ride a bike, it is incredibly hard to unlearn that simple, mildly rewarding behavior."[35]

"[Nicotine is] almost a guaranteed addiction. Some people can drink alcohol without developing a problem, not everyone who takes opiates recreationally has a problem, but pretty much everyone likes the feeling of nicotine."[34]

—Judith Grisel, neuroscientist and author of *Never Enough: The Neuroscience and Experience of Addiction*

Vaping on Planes

Vaping on planes to and from the United States is illegal, but some people choose to do it anyhow. E-cigarettes are allowed in carry-on luggage, but their use and charging of the lithium battery are both prohibited. Regulations are in place to protect other passengers from the toxins in the secondhand aerosol as well as to prevent fire from the lithium battery. Penalties include fines of up to $4,000 and jail time if smoke detectors are tampered with, or if the passenger gives crew members a hard time when confronted about vaping. Airlines also have the discretion to ban people for life from flying with them. Despite these risks, some passengers with a vaping addiction are willing to take the pull anyway.

Part of substance addiction is to continue use even in the face of negative consequences. For example, Val, a thirty-year-old designer, admits that she always vapes while she flies. In June 2019, she told an interviewer, "I know I shouldn't, and I envision the fire alarm going off and how screwed I'd be." She says that when she wants a big inhale, she exhales the vapor strongly into the toilet bowl while she flushes.

Anna Silman, "Everyone Is Vaping on the Plane," The Cut, June 20, 2019. www.thecut.com.

Tough to Quit

Some e-cigarette users become addicted at a young age. Savannah West became addicted to vaping after only a few times when she was sixteen years old. By the second week of using, she reported that her urge to vape turned into more of a need. While at school, she recounts becoming agitated if she had gone too long without it and would leave class to vape. After a year of vaping, she said that she needed it just to feel normal. Although she has tried to stop many times, West reports that she continues to vape four years later. Her message to young people considering vaping is: "Don't do it. It isn't cool, or smart. It isn't anything and it is not worth the addiction."[36]

When vapers like West try to quit, they find that they have become physically dependent on nicotine. Almost immediately they experience significant withdrawal symptoms, which peak somewhere between one and three days of last use. These symptoms include nicotine cravings, sweating, tremors, headaches, insomnia, increased appetite, abdominal cramping, and constipation. After three days, though, the nicotine is gone from the body. People still experience the strong desire to use e-cigarettes, however, because the vaping addiction is about more than nicotine.

When Vaping Becomes Habit

Vaping is not just physically addictive. It also becomes habit. People are creatures of habit and establish routines throughout the day. Daily life is fraught with triggers that make smokers and vapers feel like using not just for the nicotine, but because they associate doing so with certain activities. They might be inclined, for example, to vape after meals, while taking a break from work, talk-

Daily life is fraught with triggers that make vapers feel like using not just for the nicotine, but because they associate doing so with certain activities. They might be inclined, for example, to vape after meals.

ing on the phone, driving in a car, or simply because they are tired or bored. Every time one of these triggers occurs, people with a vaping addiction associate that moment with their e-cigarette. The connection between the trigger and the nicotine drives the habit. The National Institute on Drug Abuse explains nicotine's habitual addictive power: "The amount of dopamine released with any given puff of a cigarette is not that great compared to other drugs, but the fact that the activity is repeated so often, and in conjunction with so many other activities, ties nicotine's rewards strongly to many behaviors that we perform on a daily basis."[37]

Stephanie Beidman, a substance abuse counselor in Washington, used to smoke cigarettes. Then she switched to e-cigarettes. She had been vaping for eleven years when the news of vaping-related lung damage began making headlines. That is when she decided to quit vaping, but it was not an easy habit to break. Everywhere she went, she says, she saw people vaping—and that triggered her own strong need for e-cigarettes. In her view, vaping is more addictive than traditional cigarettes. She comments: "It's so much more socially acceptable because everybody is doing it everywhere you go even inside buildings."[38] After two months of being e-cigarette-free, she says she still craves it every time she feels stressed or is in a social setting.

> "It's like my phone. It's the same addictive quality as my phone, as like I just expect to have it in my pocket, and I miss having it in a pocket to do something with."[39]
>
> —Sydney Kinsey, twenty-one-year-old former JUUL user

Sydney Kinsey, a twenty-one-year-old student at New York University, also quit her e-cigarette habit. In order to stop smoking, she started vaping in June 2019. Realizing that she was "non-stop Juuling up a storm," and amid the EVALI incidences, Kinsey threw her JUUL in the city garbage. She misses it, though. Vaping had become part of her daily routine. In a 2019 interview she says, "It's like my phone. It's the same addictive quality as my phone, as like I just expect to have it in my pocket, and I miss having it in a pocket to do something with."[39]

Serving Size

Many users claim that e-cigarettes are also more addictive than traditional cigarettes because there is not a definitive serving size. This can lead to a higher intake of nicotine. People who vape claim that there is not a natural ending point for a vaping session. Some attest to inhaling the vapor until their hands are shaking and they feel sick. Others report draining a pod, containing roughly the same amount of nicotine found in a pack of cigarettes, in just a couple of hours. On the other hand, the serving size of one cigarette is predetermined for smokers. When smokers feel a trigger-like stress, they reach for their pack of cigarettes, pull one out, spark a lighter, ignite the end, and smoke it down to the filter. After that, the smoker is usually satiated for a period of time. This is not usually the case for e-cigarette users.

Many users claim that vaping is more addictive than cigarettes because there is not a definitive serving size. Unlike a cigarette which burns out, there is not a natural ending point when vaping.

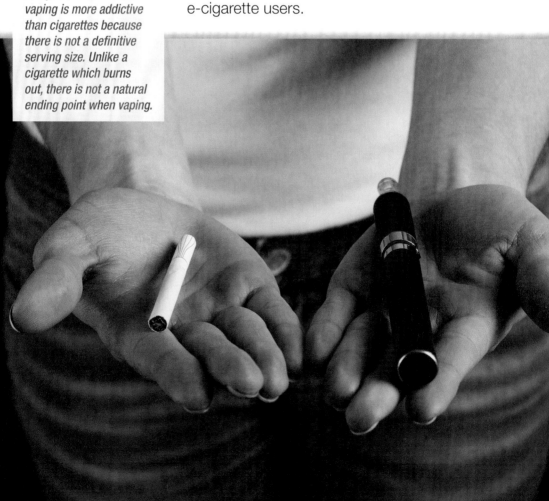

When serving sizes are vague, people consume more. Nutritionists encourage people to measure their food and be cognizant of how much they eat to avoid overconsumption. When people want to snack on almonds, for example, nutritionists recommend that they portion them out into their hand to get one ounce, which is a serving size. If they sit in front of the television with a bag of almonds in their lap, they are likely to consume much more than an ounce. Similarly, vapers are likely to consume more nicotine because it seems bottomless. In an online discussion forum, a vaper was having problems with the serving size issue. This person wrote, "I have a hard time regulating my intake. . . . It is too easy to just keep taking 'one more pull' from the vaper, until I notice my hand is shaking from the nicotine."[40] Other people on the forum recommended pods with lower nicotine levels.

The Manufacturers' Role in Addiction

Before JUUL entered the market in 2015, the most common e-cigarette products had a nicotine content of between 1 and 2.4 percent. By October 2019, JUUL had 64.4 percent of the e-cigarette market, according to Nielsen, a market research firm. The nicotine content of the JUUL pods is 5 percent, but following their inception, they began offering a 3 percent variation as well. JUUL has stated that it offers the 5 percent nicotine concentration in its pods "to provide adult smokers with a viable, satisfying alternative to combustible cigarettes."[41] These pods are equivalent to about a pack of cigarettes' worth of nicotine. JUUL also boasts that its nicotine salt formulation increases the rate of nicotine delivery, bringing it to the user's brain 2.7 times faster than other e-cigarette brands and making it easier to inhale without coughing or gagging.

As with nicotine content and salt formulation, the sleek flash drive–like design of the JUUL vaping device is aimed at increasing user appeal. Many suggest that its discreet puffs of smoke and small size make it easier to use frequently and in a lot of places. Ahmed Kabil argues, "Its pod-based delivery system and discreet design appeal to those who disdain vape culture and its appurtenances." Kabil, a former smoker, always carries his JUUL and reports using it frequently. In a December 2018 article he writes, "Over time, I realized I was Juuling far more than I ever smoked. I Juuled at my desk, in the bathroom, on the phone, at the dinner table, and while lying in bed."[42]

E-juice flavors for e-cigarettes have also captivated a large audience, many of them quite young. Flavors vary by brand, and some have been pulled from the shelves to deter underage use. There are delicious-sounding varieties such as "Mango," "Mint," "I love cookies," and "Unicorn milk." While there is little if anything appealing about the smell of a burning cigarette to a new user, a shocking number of young people have flocked to try all the flavor varieties of e-cigarettes. A 2019 study in the journal *Pediatrics* found that most of the youngest consumers were completely unaware that these pods even contained nicotine.

Teen Susceptibility to Addiction

Teens' lack of awareness of the nicotine content in e-cigarettes is especially problematic because young people are more susceptible to addiction than adults. The adolescent brain is more sensitive to the reward center and its release of dopamine. Yale neuroscientist Marina Picciotto argues, "Adolescents don't think they will get addicted to nicotine, but when they do want to stop, they find it's very difficult."[43]

Young people who vape are at higher risk than are adults of damage to the part of their brain that affects attention span, learning, mood, and impulse control. The brain is not finished growing until people are in their mid- to late twenties. The developing brain quickly builds synapses that act as bridges between brain cells. These synapses are made when people learn new things, like playing a musical instrument. But these productive synapses are essentially hijacked with exposure to an addictive substance like nicotine. Synapses facilitate learning and create memories. But they can be disrupted by nicotine, thereby impacting one's ability to learn and create memories.

The Financial Cost of Vaping Addiction for Teens

For teens with e-cigarette addictions, the costs can add up quickly. Vaping is prohibited by law nationwide for anyone under the age of twenty-one. This has resulted in third-party dealers who buy pods legitimately either online or in stores and sell them to teens at a higher price. The cost to underage users is often twice as high as the cost to legal buyers. Many teens report vaping about four pods per week. Depending on which pods they prefer and where they buy them, teens pay from $1,000 to $1,500 annually to maintain their addiction.

Sophie, a nineteen-year-old studying at the University of Vermont who makes about $200 a week delivering pizzas, says she spends most of her extra money on JUUL pods. In a June 2019 interview, Sophie said, "I spend $25 a week on pods, which is pretty common for people that Juul often, but there are definitely people that spend more." After vaping for two years, she said she is not trying to quit, but wishes that she never started.

James Wellemeyer, "Teens Can Spend $1,000 per Year on Vaping," MarketWatch, June 29, 2019. www.marketwatch.com.

Although it is not legal to vape until the person is twenty-one years old, teens are surrounded by e-cigarettes in and out of school. In 2019 Caleb Mintz, seventeen, described the epidemic of vaping addiction around him. He says, "It's not really even a social thing anymore. People are just doing it alone, and it's just to get by."[44]

Vaping nicotine is highly addictive in both substance and habit. Manufacturers arguably have contributed to vaping's addictive power. An e-cigarette's sleek design, high nicotine content, smooth salt formulation, and variety of aerosol flavors have attracted millions of users—too many of them underage—and kept them coming back for more.

CHAPTER FOUR

Cracking Down on Marketing and Teen Use

There has been some speculation that e-cigarette companies intentionally try to appeal to young people. JUUL in particular is under public scrutiny for allegedly marketing its product directly to teenagers. The *New York Times* reports that in 2018 JUUL paid $10,000 to schools that implemented an antismoking program. Six schools agreed to the five-year program, which used a company-sponsored curriculum that included the teachers leaving their classrooms so that the students would feel safer about speaking honestly. While JUUL representatives claim the programs were meant to educate teens about tobacco addiction and prevention, critics argue the company used the program for marketing their products. In July 2019, Caleb Mintz, seventeen, testified in front of a US House of Representatives panel that a representative of JUUL visited his New York high school in April 2018. When there was not a teacher present, Mintz claims that the JUUL representative told the students that the vaping device was "totally safe" and showed them how to use it. He says, "For my classmates who were already vaping, it was a sigh of relief because now they were able to vape without any concern."[45]

JUUL's chief administrative officer Ashley Gould said that the company ended the program shortly after its inception because it was not well received, and that its intentions were misinterpreted. Despite mounting evidence of JUUL's alleged targeted appeal to teens, in March 2018, JUUL spokesperson Christine Castro claimed, "This product is solely for adult smokers. We absolutely condemn kids using our products."[46]

> "This product is solely for adult smokers. We absolutely condemn kids using our products."[46]
>
> —Christine Castro, JUUL spokesperson

Influencers Appeal to Teens

Statements from top e-cigarette company representatives would indicate that they are not trying to market to teens, but their social media platforms suggest otherwise. JUUL, for example, spent over $1 million on advertising campaigns on Twitter, Instagram,

In 2018, JUUL paid $10,000 to schools that implemented an antismoking program. Critics, as well as some students, argue the company used the program for marketing their products to teenagers.

and YouTube. Many of these ads featured young people using their product. Others featured brand influencers known to appeal to young people. A 2019 *Psychology Today* article suggests that this type of advertising can lead to more young people using e-cigarettes. Public health specialist Michele Ybarra writes, "Unregulated advertising of e-cigarettes to youth through social media and advertising campaigns elsewhere can lead to the glamorization of vaping among young people; and this could lead to their use."[47]

Christina Zayas, thirty-six, was one of the influencers that JUUL contacted to advertise on Instagram. The company asked her in an email to try JUUL's product and share her experience on her social media platform. Zayas explains why they selected her in particular: "They liked my edgy style and that I appealed to the younger market."[48] In November 2017, on Instagram she posted a picture of herself vaping along with her impressions of JUUL. The post reached 4,500 people and got about 1,500 likes. In return, JUUL paid her $1,000. In November 2018, the company suspended most of its social media marketing campaigns under increasing public pressure associated with the rising number of teens who vape.

> "Unregulated advertising of e-cigarettes to youth through social media and advertising campaigns elsewhere can lead to the glamorization of vaping among young people; and this could lead to their use."[47]
>
> —Michele Ybarra, public health specialist

But by then many teens had already bought into JUUL's message. As a fifteen-year-old sophomore in a Florida high school, Bailey Legacki was enticed into smoking e-cigarettes, specifically JUUL, because of its social media marketing campaign and the product's ubiquitous presence. Regarding the marketing campaign, she tells the *New York Times*, "They were young people and it looked like they were having fun. Or, it would just be the device that was shown, but not really explaining anything about it just, 'Try this'."[49] Legacki did not realize that e-cigarettes had nicotine and claims that she would not have started vaping if she had known. Now eighteen years old and unable to quit vaping, Legacki is suing JUUL.

Vaping at School

Vaping is rampant in many schools. Sharon Levy, director of the Adolescent Substance Use and Addiction Program at Boston Children's Hospital, says, "I have kids who were doing well over the summer and were saying, 'I don't want to go back to school, because I know I'm going to walk into the bathroom and everybody's going to be handing me a Juul'."

High school students, and even some middle school students, are vaping in bathrooms, empty hallways, and the back of classrooms across the United States. School administrators are taking action to stop this trend, but it is an uphill battle. A Montgomery County, Pennsylvania, school district banned the use of flash drives because JUUL vape devices too closely resembled them. The school officials hoped to make concealing them more difficult for teens. Meanwhile, a school in Lauderdale County, Alabama, removed doors from its bathroom stalls to deter e-cigarette users. Other schools have installed sensors to detect the use of e-cigarettes in bathrooms and locker rooms. Vaping at school has become such a pervasive issue that many students refer to school restrooms as "the JUUL room."

Sara Harrison, "So You Want to Quit Vaping? No One Actually Knows How," *Wired*, October 4, 2019. www.wired.com.

Legacki and her lawyer believe that e-cigarette manufacturers played a central role in the teen vaping addiction epidemic—and they are not alone in that view. In November 2019, *New York Times* investigative reporters Julie Creswell and Sheila Kaplan wrote, "Juul planted the seeds of a public health crisis by marketing to millennials, who had low smoking rates, and it ignored evidence that teenagers were using its products."[50]

Favorite Flavors

According to the CDC, teen use of e-cigarettes rose from 11.7 percent of high school students in 2017 to 27.5 percent in 2019.

In an effort to understand the reasons behind this large increase, analysts have studied marketing techniques and also teen e-juice flavor preferences. An academic article published in the August 2018 journal PLoS ONE suggests that "the wide variety of flavors available and the freedom to 'mix-and-match' flavors may maintain use of e-cigarettes among youth and adults."[51] The same study found that young people prefer the sweeter fruit and candy flavors. A subsequent study published in the November 2019 issue of the *Journal of the American Medical Association* found that the eighth, tenth, and twelfth graders surveyed preferred the mango and mint flavors the most. After the data revealed that 60 percent of the high school e-cigarette users prefer mint, JUUL stopped the sale of mint-flavored pods.

Public response to the findings that e-cigarette use is so prevalent among teens, and that flavor selection likely

A study indicated that the variety of e-juice flavors available may maintain use of e-cigarettes among youth and adults. The same study found that young people prefer the sweeter fruit and candy flavors.

plays a role in that, led to a widespread outcry for federal regulation. Policy makers heard the collective voice of parents and health experts across the country. During a July 2019 congressional hearing on JUUL's youth marketing practices, US representative Mark DeSaulnier from California told the cofounder of JUUL Labs, James Monsees: "You're nothing but a marketer of poison and your target has been young people."[52] First Lady Melania Trump also supported more regulation to prevent teen use. In a September 2019 tweet, she emphasized the role that parents play in the fight against teen vaping and stated that the Trump administration supports removing flavored e-cigarettes from stores unless they receive FDA approval.

On February 5, 2020, the federal government ruled that all new flavors must be approved by the FDA. Flavors already being marketed, even those that have been shown to appeal to teens, can continue to be sold, pending FDA review.

There is also widespread concern that teens will be switching to disposable vapes that entered the market in the spring of 2019. Called *pod-mods*, they resemble the JUUL vape device and come in a variety of sweet flavors (such as pink lemonade) that mask the harshness of tobacco. Cristine Delnevo, director of the Center for Tobacco Studies at Rutgers University, explains that regulation has a challenge in keeping up with the market. She says, "It's a bit of a game of whack-a-mole, so when policies are aimed at one product, another product pops-up to fill the void."[53]

Legal Age Is Twenty-One

Aside from the flavor ban, the federal government is implementing laws to restrict young people's access to e-cigarettes. On December 20, 2019, President Trump signed a bill into law that increased the age for using and purchasing tobacco products, including e-cigarettes and vaping devices, from eighteen to twenty-one. Senator Mitch McConnell spoke in favor of the bipartisan legislation he cosponsored with Senator Tim Kaine when he said, "It is our responsibility as parents and public servants to do everything we can to keep these harmful products out of high schools and out of youth culture."[54]

Many experts and educational organizations, such as the National Association of Secondary School Principals (NASSP), supported the bill, hoping it would decrease the use of e-cigarettes in schools. NASSP executive director JoAnn Bartoletti argued that teen vaping is "one of the greatest public health issues our schools are facing."[55] In her address supporting the legislation, Bartoletti said that principals across the country would continue working to prevent and stop vaping in schools, and that raising the vaping age to twenty-one would help those efforts.

Some people are skeptical that increasing the legal age will make a difference. It is widely known that there was already a black market for teens under eighteen to buy vaping products before the legislation passed. Those of age purchase e-cigarettes and vaping paraphernalia in bulk and sell it to younger people for a premium. Ali Yaz, who manages a vaping store in Seattle, says, "I don't think it's gonna make any difference for the kids."[56]

"It is our responsibility as parents and public servants to do everything we can to keep these harmful products out of high schools and out of youth culture."[54]

—Mitch McConnell, US senator

On the other hand, many people believe raising the legal age will reduce the number of teens who vape. Aneesa Roidad, a senior at Ballard High School in Seattle, reports that students are always vaping in the high school bathrooms. Roidad believes the legislation is a productive step toward curbing teen vaping. "I don't smoke or vape myself," she says, "but I do think it would be easier to ask a senior or a friend than find someone who is 21."[57]

The legal vaping age is inconsequential if vaping vendors, both brick and mortar and those online, sell to underage customers. The FDA has begun using compliance officers under the age of twenty-one to attempt to buy tobacco and vaping products from retailers. Retailers are expected to verify the age of anyone who looks

FUTURE ~ VAPOR

An employee at a vape shop talks with a customer. Retailers selling vaping products are expected to verify the age of anyone who looks like they are under twenty-seven years old.

like they are under twenty-seven years old. If retailers sell to underage customers during the compliance check, the FDA sends the retailer a Compliance Check Inspection Notice. It is up to the states to enforce the legal age both in sales and use, so penalties for the vendors and underage users vary by state.

The legal-age increase prompted many states to introduce bills specifying how they would enforce the law. Legislation under consideration in Georgia, for example, would make the third and subsequent violations of private sales of vaping and e-cigarette products to underage users a felony. Indiana is considering legislation at the state level which would revoke a retailer's tobacco license for three years following their third offense of underage sales.

Vaping in "Party Mode"

A feature of a JUUL vaping device that arguably attracts young people is its bright blinking lights when switched to "party mode." JUUL manufacturers quietly slipped the feature into the device for its consumers to discover. The vaper takes a hit, waits for the white line to glow, and then shakes it aggressively back and forth to get all of the colors blinking. People use it to get attention at a party, dance club, or concert. Teens report sharing their JUULs at these events. Vaping in party mode signals to all the people in the area that there is a JUUL present. Cornell University student Jason Jeong describes a common scenario: "Someone pulls one out at a party, and naturally the question is 'Can I try it?,' and then after 'Can I try it?' five or six times you end up buying your own, and, soon enough, you're breathing in more Juul than air."

Quoted in Jia Tolentino, "The Promise of Vaping and the Rise of Juul," *New Yorker*, May 14, 2018. www.newyorker.com.

Sometimes vendors take calculated risks. Depending on the penalties, some would rather continue selling to minors and risk getting caught by a compliance officer than turn teens away and reduce their sales. Teens report knowing which vendors they can frequent to buy vaping products. After California had raised its legal tobacco and vaping age to twenty-one, CNN reported that a June 2019 undercover operation in California revealed that only half of the vape shops visited required underage customers to show ID.

E-Cigarettes as a Gateway to Cigarettes

State and federal governments are enacting laws aimed at teen vaping for many reasons. Among them, research suggests that vaping is a gateway to traditional cigarettes. In a July 2019 news release, acting FDA commissioner Ned Sharpless explains,

"Teens who vape are more likely to start smoking cigarettes, putting them at risk of a lifetime of addiction to smoking and related disease."[58]

In August 2019, shortly after the FDA publicly linked e-cigarettes and traditional cigarettes, JUUL's CEO Kevin Burns made his own public statements on the link between the two. He urged people who did not smoke cigarettes in the past to not start vaping. He said, "Don't vape. Don't use JUUL. Don't start using nicotine if you don't have a preexisting relationship with nicotine. Don't use the product. You're not our target consumer."[59]

Some teens have tried e-cigarettes because they did have a preexisting relationship with nicotine. Many of the young people who started using e-cigarettes to quit smoking report that they once again picked up cigarettes to stop vaping. Lucas McClain of Arlington, Virginia, is among them. He began smoking traditional cigarettes in high school and switched to e-cigarettes because he thought it was a safer alternative. But he says that e-cigarettes, JUUL in particular, made his nicotine addiction worse. He could finish a pod, equivalent to about a pack of cigarettes' worth of nicotine, in three hours. "When I didn't have it for more than two hours, I'd get very anxious," he told NBC News.[60] McClain knows the risks of cigarettes—lung cancer even runs in his family. But he thinks it will be easier for him to quit smoking than vaping.

It is increasingly apparent that vaping and e-cigarette use are addictive and harmful for anyone, but especially for teens and young adults. The reason that the issue of e-cigarette and vaping risks has risen to national prominence, however, is not just because it is harmful, but because the face of this particular addiction is very young. The nation's parents, health practitioners, and policy makers are collectively distressed that young people are at the front lines of this epidemic.

> "Teens who vape are more likely to start smoking cigarettes, putting them at risk of a lifetime of addiction to smoking and related disease."[58]
>
> —Ned Sharpless, acting FDA commissioner

CHAPTER FIVE

Kicking the Habit

Vaping is often touted as a safer alternative to smoking cigarettes, but many people argue that it is more difficult to quit vaping than smoking. Luka Kinard, a sixteen-year-old high school junior, was so addicted that he needed inpatient rehabilitation to stop vaping. He began using e-cigarettes when he was fourteen years old at a high school football game. At first, he tried it to fit in and then as a stress reliever. But then he found himself completely addicted and spending $150 per week on JUUL pods. In an October 2019 interview, he explains, "As you get up in the morning, the first thing you do, instead of brushing your teeth or, you know, getting out of bed, is you get your morning buzz. So, you hit your vape. And then, at school . . . you do it in the classroom, you do it in the bathrooms."[61] Kinard was a straight-A student, but started failing his classes and missing extracurricular activities after he started vaping.

> "[High school] just wasn't a healthy environment for me to be sober."[62]
>
> —Luka Kinard, attended inpatient rehabilitation at age sixteen to quit vaping

In September 2019, Kinard had a seizure and his parents decided he needed drastic intervention to help him stop vaping. He spent 39 days in an inpatient rehabilitation program that included group sessions and one-on-one therapy. The groups focused on sobriety, self-awareness, and healthier ways to communicate. When Kinard finished the time in rehab and had successfully stopped vaping, he went back to school. Because of the ubiquitous presence of e-cigarettes, he reports, "[High school] just wasn't a healthy environment for me to be sober."[62] To maintain his sobriety and have a flexible schedule, he opts for online classes.

Quitting Is More Challenging for Teens than Adults

Quitting for teens in high school is arguably more challenging than for others who vape because e-cigarette use seems to be everywhere they turn—in the bathrooms and even in the classrooms. Kamal Mazhar, a high school senior in Virginia who does not vape, told *Time* in January 2020 that one time when he went to use the school restroom, he found a dozen students vaping together in two bathroom stalls.

A Truth Initiative survey published in January 2020 finds that half of the fifteen- to twenty-four-year-olds who vape made

Some young adults become addicted to vaping, letting it control their lives. Rehabilitation programs that include group therapy can help foster sobriety, self-awareness, and healthier ways to communicate.

quitting their New Year's resolution. Truth Initiative further reports that teens who try to stop vaping say that they face social isolation and sometimes bullying at school. Many of them claim that they are the only one in their social group trying to quit. Phoebe Chambers, a high school junior in Maryland, explains why suggesting that teens should find a different social circle would not help. In an October 2019 interview, she said, "[Vaping's] not just something that's limited to one social group. It's not just like the group of kids who, like, are stoners. It's the athletes. It's the nerds. It's everybody."[63] Even with the strong pull of addiction and social pressure, though, teens and adults alike are trying a variety of methods to put down their e-cigarettes once and for all.

For many people addicted to vaping, inpatient rehabilitation is not an option. It is both expensive and time-consuming. The first step to which many e-cigarette users turn is getting a prescription to address the nicotine addiction. They might use a variety of nicotine replacement therapy techniques, such as nicotine gum and patches, as well as medications, such as varenicline, to reduce the cravings and pleasurable effects of nicotine. In many cases, though, vaping is about more than a nicotine addiction, and users find these techniques insufficient by themselves.

Behavioral Replacements

In part, vaping is a behavioral addiction much like cell phone use. E-cigarette users vape when they are bored, have a break, drink a coffee, have a meal, feel tired, and during a variety of other moments in a day. People committed to quitting need a way to replace vaping with a different activity. Some report chewing on straws. Stephanie Beidman, who was especially fond of all the flavor pods, says she bought twenty packs of flavored gum and put them everywhere—in her car, house, and office. She explains that every time she had the urge to vape, she grabbed a different flavor of gum to chew.

People committed to quitting need a way to replace vaping with a different activity. Some chew on straws or keep a wide variety of flavors of chewing gum around to satisfy their urges to vape.

Henry Korman, who had replaced his smoking habit with vaping, put down his JUUL for good in September 2019. He decided to be healthier and also realized his JUUL habit was costing him eight dollars per day. Korman says he began eating sugar snap peas to stop vaping. Rather than his JUUL, he carries a large bag of the legumes with him, eating one every time he feels like vaping. He goes through a pound of them a week. He says, "I used to say 'phone, keys, wallet, Juul'—that's what I needed to have before I left the house. But now it's 'phone, keys, wallet, peas.'"[64]

Jamie Putnam used cinnamon-flavored toothpicks and a four-sided fidget cube to quit vaping. She had started smoking cigarettes at thirteen years old and used vaping as a smoking replacement nine years later. When the

"I used to say 'phone, keys, wallet, Juul'—that's what I needed to have before I left the house. But now it's 'phone, keys, wallet, peas.'"[64]

—Henry Korman, used sugar snap peas to stop vaping

COVID-19: Another Reason to Quit Vaping

The highly contagious coronavirus disease, COVID-19, has resulted in hundreds of thousands of deaths and hospitalizations across the world. Long-term data on the relationship between vaping and COVID-19 is not available because the first case presented itself in Wuhan, China, in December 2019. Because the virus attacks the respiratory system, however, medical experts believe that those who vape and smoke are at a higher risk of serious complications. Medical experts have noticed a higher rate of complications and death from COVID-19 among Chinese men than women. One possible explanation for this is that more men than women smoke in China. Additionally, a study in the *Chinese Medical Journal* found that of seventy-eight COVID-19 patients, those with a history of smoking were fourteen times as likely to develop pneumonia.

Medical experts also suggest that vaping increases susceptibility to COVID-19 as well as worsens its consequences because the aerosols seem to hurt pulmonary cells and the lungs are unable to clear the secretions. At the height of the pandemic, in March 2020, Dr. Dean Drosnes, the medical director of the Pennsylvania campus of Caron Treatment Centers, commented, "If you are looking to stop vaping, it's a great time to stop."

David Levine, "Does Smoking and Vaping Make Coronavirus Worse?," *U.S. News & World Report*, March 31, 2020. https://health.usnews.com.

EVALI incidences filled the headlines in 2019, she decided to stop vaping. Aside from keeping her hands and mouth busy, Putnam explains in an article in Everyday Health that a key component to her success was to create accountability by picking a quit day and letting her friends and family know. She writes, "I told my boyfriend, my friends, my parents, and my coworkers. Just having people around me know what I was going through helped to hold me accountable."[65]

Social Support

Breaking an addiction is difficult. Doing it alone can feel impossible. A large body of research shows that recovery from addiction is more likely if the addict has support. In the *Harvard Gazette*, Sue McGreevey explains that recovery programs like Alcoholics Anonymous are helpful to deal with addiction for many reasons. Among them, she argues, two are the most important: "spending more time with individuals who support efforts toward sobriety and increased confidence in the ability to maintain abstinence in social situations."[66]

Some young people feel alone in their journeys to quit vaping. They are afraid to tell their parents that they ever started vaping in the first place. Often they do not get the support they need from their friends at school who continue to use e-cigarettes. For these reasons, in January 2019, Truth Initiative, a nonprofit public health organization committed to ending vaping and smoking, launched a free mobile texting program called "This Is Quitting." For eight weeks, the program sends daily text messages for motivation, inspiration, and support while young people, ages thirteen to twenty-four, stop vaping. Participants can text key words such as COPE, STRESS, SLIP, or MORE for immediate messages if they are experiencing increased urges to use their e-cigarette.

"They make it seem like there is a way out of addiction."[67]

—Chase, a teen who used Truth Initiative to help him stop vaping

Many young people have found Truth Initiative helpful. Chase, a teen who used the program, offers a testimonial on its website: "They make it seem like there is a way out of addiction."[67] Nicotine and tobacco research from Truth Initiative reports that in 2019, seventy thousand young people enrolled in This Is Quitting. After two weeks in the program, 60.8 percent of the participants revealed that they had either quit or reduced their vaping habit.

Cold Turkey or Weaning

While some people choose a day to quit and stop their use completely—referred to as "going cold turkey"—others decrease frequency of use or nicotine content over time. Indra Cidambi, addiction psychiatrist and medical director at the Center for Network Therapy, argues that for some people weaning is an effective method for quitting, but it requires planning. Cidambi advises, "Pay attention to how many times a day you're using it. Then try to give yourself some structure."[68] For example, if people use their e-cigarette ten times a day, they could aim to reduce it each week by two times per day. Additionally, people on 5-percent-nicotine pods can use lower doses over time.

There are several accounts of young people going cold turkey on TikTok under #ThisIsQuitting. Some are recording themselves throwing their vapes out the window, and others are submerging them in water so they no longer work. Tisha Alyn, a professional golfer, dancer, fitness model, and broadcaster, has used her social media platform to encourage people to quit vaping. In Alyn's video, she uses a golf club to flip a vape into a glass of ice water that her friend is holding up. In January 2020, she told an interviewer, "I'm very excited to partner with truth and use my platform to inspire kids to kick their JUULs to the curb and quit for good."[69]

"I'm very excited to partner with truth and use my platform to inspire kids to kick their JUULs to the curb and quit for good."[69]

—Tisha Alyn, professional golfer

Other social media influencers have joined the campaign to encourage young people to quit. Samuel Grubbs, for example, posted a video on TikTok in which he and a group of friends destroyed their vaping devices with fluid coming out of exploding soda bottles. Similarly, Nick Uhas, an actor, posted a video on TikTok in which he voluntarily ruins his vaping device in the chemical used in heating pads. Uhas recognizes the power that social media had in influencing teens to vape and suggests wielding that power to deter them. He says, "You have to go through the same tactics. It's wise to go where the eyeballs are looking."[70]

While some teens post on social media to demonstrate their commitment to stop vaping, others do so in a more private man-

Whether vapers wean or quit cold turkey, many experts suggest writing out a personal plan and sharing it with family and friends.

ner. Some teens report having thrown their vaping devices in the city garbage or locking them in a three-day safe to stop vaping. Whether vapers wean or quit cold turkey, many experts agree that there are a few steps they can take to make it more likely to stay off their electronic nicotine devices permanently. They suggest choosing the quit day, writing out a personal plan, telling family and friends, avoiding triggers, keeping busy, creating a different reward system, and managing food and drinks.

Relapse and Withdrawal

The addiction to nicotine and e-cigarettes is powerful. People who have a great plan and plenty of support still might relapse or start vaping again. Medical professionals report that some patients with lung injuries have been hospitalized twice for vaping. Readmissions range from five days to fifty-five days after patients were initially released. In some of the cases, patients had started vaping again after they were released from the hospital the first time.

Bella Hadid Quits Vaping

Many celebrities use e-cigarettes, which has likely made vaping more appealing to teens and young adults. Leonardo DiCaprio, Isla Fisher, and Samuel L. Jackson are among the celebrities who have vaped. Katy Perry and Orlando Bloom were seen sharing a vape pen at the Golden Globes.

But as the health consequences of vaping have become more apparent, some celebrities have committed to ditching the habit. Victoria's Secret model Bella Hadid, twenty-three, made a New Year's resolution to stop vaping in 2019. In January 2019, she posted on Instagram, "2019 resolution—quit Juuling! So far so good!" Her vaping habit had replaced her smoking habit in 2017. Hadid, who suffers from Lyme disease, told an interviewer that she wanted to focus on her health and that quitting JUUL was part of that effort. Referring to the annual Victoria's Secret fashion show, she says, "I've been really sick for the past few years, and it was really hard for me to fully experience the whole [fashion] show and have fun with it and be excited. This year I really just feel like I am myself again and happy and healthy in all aspects of my life."

Quoted in Julie Mazziotta, "Bella Hadid Gave Up E-Cigarettes for the New Year: 'So Far So Good!'" *People*, January 7, 2019. https://people.com.

Multiple hospital visits from vaping injuries highlight the need for addiction management with medical treatment. Dixie Harris, a Utah pulmonologist and critical care physician, recalls two patients who started using e-cigarettes after their first stay in the hospital with lung injuries. Harris said both patients eventually required surgery and suffered significant lung complications. Additionally, in October 2019 a seventeen-year-old boy from New York died from vaping injuries during his second hospital visit.

Doctors suggest that the underlying reasons young people vape need to be addressed to decrease their likelihood of relapse. Anne Griffiths, a pediatric pulmonologist at Children's Minnesota, tells the *Washington Post*, "Discharging children home after this lung injury without counseling or therapy or addiction management, I think, is a big mistake."[71]

Addiction management would be helpful for people who use e-cigarettes to assist them in recognizing physical and psychological withdrawal symptoms and learn techniques to cope with them. These symptoms include cravings, irritability, anxiety, mood swings, difficulty concentrating, headaches, abdominal cramps, digestive issues, sleeping problems, sweating, tremors, and weight gain. While the physical symptoms dissipate after a few days, the cravings and other psychological symptoms of addiction can continue for weeks or even months.

Considering the prolonged psychological withdrawal symptoms, relapse is not entirely surprising. In a February 2020 article, Lisa Mulcahy details what helped her quit vaping. Rather than viewing slips along the way as a sign of failure, she used them as learning opportunities. She analyzed what factors enabled her to refrain from vaping as well as the triggers that got her started again. And even when she slipped, she tried again. She did not give up.

Many medical experts further recommend that people trying to put down their vaping devices should expect that they will gain a little weight. Nicotine suppresses the appetite. When people quit vaping, they might find that they feel hungrier than before. Also, there is a need to keep the hands and mouth occupied so many people tend to eat when they get e-cigarette cravings. Based on her own experience, Mulcahy's advice to people trying to quit is the following: "Once you get through the complete process of quitting vapes, then you can focus your attention on shedding that small amount of weight. Don't take on too much at once."[72] Weight gain is often particularly worrisome for teens. But it is not permanent, and being healthy is the most important priority.

A Promising New Narrative

The promising news on the front lines of the vaping epidemic is that more teens seem to believe that being healthy means quitting vaping—and they are warning their friends. For several years, the news was bleaker. Every year, more and more teens were vaping. The number and severity of EVALI cases in emergency rooms across the nation, which peaked in September 2019, left medical professionals worried and desperate for answers. But a generation of teens that has watched school bathrooms become "JUUL rooms," witnessed themselves or their friends get sick and hospitalized from vaping, and considered that companies might be marketing to them in particular, are growing angry.

These teens are the promising new narrative of ending the vaping epidemic. In the darkest days of 2019 as their peers lay in hospital beds dying from vaping injuries and their school hallways were filled with toxic aerosol, they grew restless and decided the vaping epidemic has to stop. They formed advocacy groups like "Teens Against Vaping" and began writing congressional testimonies. They posted photos of themselves on their social media platforms with tubes down their throats in hospitals from vaping injuries with captions begging their peers to stop. They joined the movement on TikTok and posted videos where they destroyed their e-cigarettes or vaping devices under the hashtag #ThisIsQuitting. Political figures, school administrators, and parents will work together to create and implement policies to protect young people. But change will occur when teens make it happen.

Introduction: The Rise of Vaping and E-Cigarettes

1. Quoted in American Non-Smokers' Rights Foundation, "Electronic Smoking Devices and Secondhand Aerosol," 2020. https://no-smoke.org.
2. Quoted in Chesky Ron, "The Many Fathers of Vaping," Tech-Walls, June 18, 2019. www.techwalls.com.

Chapter One: A Pervasive Problem

3. Quoted in Stephanie Baer, "These Teens Were Hospitalized with Vaping Injuries. Now They're Sharing Their Stories and Helping Other Young People Quit," BuzzFeed, September 11, 2019. www.buzzfeednews.com.
4. Quoted in Hannah Sparks, "Student Shares Shocking Images of Collapsed Lung After Vaping for a Year," *New York Post*, August 8, 2019. https://nypost.com.
5. U.S. Department of Health & Human Services, "Surgeon General Releases Advisory on E-Cigarette Epidemic Among Youth," HHS.gov, December 18, 2018. www.hhs.gov.
6. Michael Blaha, "Will Vaping Lead Teens to Smoking Cigarettes?," Johns Hopkins Medicine, 2020. www.hopkinsmedicine.org.
7. JUUL, "The JUUL Community," 2020. www.juul.com.
8. Nick English, "I Started Vaping to Quit Smoking and It Was a Huge Mistake," *Men's Health*, October 22, 2018. www.menshealth.com.
9. Peter Hajek et al., "A Randomized Trial of E-Cigarettes Versus Nicotine Replacement Therapy," *New England Journal of Medicine* 380 (2019). www.nejm.org.
10. English, "I Started Vaping to Quit Smoking and It Was a Huge Mistake."
11. Robert Shmerling, "Can Vaping Help You Quit Smoking?," Harvard Health Publishing, February 27, 2019. www.health.harvard.edu.

12. Karen Wilson, Debra Black, and Leon Black, "Not Just 'Harmless Water Vapor,'" AAP News and Journals Gateway, October 15, 2019. www.aappublications.org.
13. Quoted in Baer, "These Teens Were Hospitalized with Vaping Injuries."

Chapter Two: Consequences of Vaping

14. Quoted in Tamar Lapin and Craig McCarthy, "Teen Who Was First New Yorker to Die in Vaping-Related Illness Named," *New York Post*, December 18, 2019. https://nypost.com.
15. Quoted in Denise Grady, "Vaping Kills a 15-Year-Old in Texas," *New York Times*, January 9, 2020. www.nytimes.com.
16. Quoted in Shira Feder, "A Teen Had a Double Lung Transplant due to Vaping-Related Lung Damage," Insider, February 5, 2020. www.insider.com.
17. KTRK-TV, "Former Teenaged Vape User Speaks Out After Double Lung Transplant," ABC13 Eyewitness News, January 31, 2020. https://abc13.com.
18. Michael Blaha, "5 Vaping Facts You Need to Know," Johns Hopkins Medicine, www.hopkinsmedicine.org.
19. CDC, "Outbreak of Lung Injury Associated with E-Cigarettes or Vaping Products," February 25, 2020. www.cdc.gov.
20. Rachael Rettner, "A Teen in Canada May Be the First Vaping Victim to Develop This Rare Lung Injury," LiveScience, November 21, 2019. www.livescience.com.
21. S.T. Landman et al., "Life-Threatening Bronchiolitis Related to Electronic Cigarette Use in a Canadian Youth," *Canadian Medical Association Journal* 191, no. 48 (December 2, 2019). www.ncbi.nlm.nih.gov.
22. Robert Shmerling, "Can Vaping Damage Your Lungs? What We Do (and Don't) Know," Harvard Health Publishing, September 4, 2019. www.health.harvard.edu.
23. Linda Carroll, "Vaping May Disrupt Immune Cells in the Lungs, Mouse Study Finds," NBC News, September 4, 2019. www.nbcnews.com.
24. Sally Hawkins et al., "Teen Who Was Put on Life-Support for Vaping Says 'I Didn't Think of Myself as a Smoker,'" NBC News, September 11, 2019. https://abcnews.go.com.

25. Marin Kuntic et al., "Short-Term E-Cigarette Vapour Exposure Causes Vascular Oxidative Stress and Dysfunction," *European Heart Journal*, November 13, 2019. https://academic.oup.com.
26. Quoted in Gemma Mullin, "Dad-of-Four, 49, Blames Vaping for Heart Attack After He Quit Smoking," *The Sun*, December 3, 2019. www.the-sun.com.
27. Quoted in Mullin, "Dad-of-Four, 49, Blames Vaping for Heart Attack After He Quit Smoking."
28. Quoted in Brendon Stiles and Steve Alperin, "We Ignored the Evidence Linking Cigarettes to Cancer. Let's Not Do That with Vaping," *The Guardian*, February 16, 2019. www.theguardian.com.
29. Stiles and Alperin, "We Ignored the Evidence Linking Cigarettes to Cancer."
30. Quoted in Denise Grady, "Lung Damage from Vaping Resembles Chemical Burns, Report Says," *New York Times*, October 2, 2019. www.nytimes.com.

Chapter Three: Addicted to Vaping

31. Kari Paul, "Breaking Up with My Juul: Why Quitting Vaping Is Harder than Quitting Cigarettes," *The Guardian*, October 10, 2019. www.theguardian.com.
32. Paul, "Breaking Up with My Juul."
33. Quoted in Paul, "Breaking Up with My Juul."
34. Quoted in Paul, "Breaking Up with My Juul."
35. National Institute on Drug Abuse, "Recent Research Sheds New Light on Why Nicotine Is So Addictive," September 28, 2018. www.drugabuse.gov.
36. Quoted in Beasley Allen Law Firm, "She Felt That She Needed to Vape 'Just to Feel Normal' Physically," *USA Today*, October 15, 2019. www.usatoday.com.
37. "Recent Research Sheds New Light on Why Nicotine Is So Addictive," National Institute on Drug Abuse, September 28, 2018. www.drugabuse.gov.
38. Quoted in Lauren Kahl, "Former Vaping Addict Warns Others at Town Hall," KLEW TV, December 12, 2019. https://klewtv.com.

39. Quoted in Eric Levenson, "'I Was Non-Stop Juuling Up a Storm': 10 College Students on Their Vaping Addictions," CNN, September 15, 2019. www.cnn.com.
40. bridgebones, "How Do You Regulate Serving Size When You Vape?," r/electronic_cigarette, Reddit. April 10, 2015. www.reddit.com.
41. Quoted in Paul, "Breaking Up with My Juul."
42. Ahmed Kabil, "Confessions of a Juul Junkie," GEN, Medium, December 4, 2018. https://gen.medium.com.
43. Quoted in Kathleen Raven, "Nicotine Addiction from Vaping Is a Bigger Problem Than Teens Realize," Yale Medicine, March 19, 2019. www.yalemedicine.org.
44. Quoted in Justin Thompson-Gee, "Vaping Has Created Teen Nicotine Addicts with Few Treatment Options," CBS News, January 18, 2019. www.cbs58.com.

Chapter Four: Cracking Down on Marketing and Teen Use

45. Quoted in Erika Edwards, "Juul Comes Under Fire for Allegedly Hijacking Teen Anti-Smoking Curriculum," NBC News, July 25, 2019. www.nbcnews.com.
46. Quoted in Ana Ibarra, "The Juul's So Cool, Kids Smoke It in School," Kaiser Health News, March 26, 2018. https://khn.org.
47. Michele Ybarra, "The Influence of Social Media on Teen Use of E-Cigarettes," *Psychology Today*, March 21, 2019. www.psychologytoday.com.
48. Michael Nedelman, Roni Selig, and Arman Azad, "#JUUL: How Social Media Hyped Nicotine for a New Generation," CNN, December 19, 2018. www.cnn.com.
49. Quoted in Julie Creswell and Sheila Kaplan, "How Juul Hooked a Generation on Nicotine," *New York Times*, November 23, 2019. www.nytimes.com.
50. Creswell and Kaplan, "How Juul Hooked a Generation on Nicotine."
51. Liane M. Schneller LM et al., "Use of Flavored Electronic Cigarette Refill Liquids Among Adults and Youth in the US— Results from Wave 2 of the Population Assessment of To-

bacco and Health Study (2014–2015)," PLoS ONE 13, no. 8 (August 23, 2018), e0202744. https://doi.org.

52. Quoted in Edwards, "Juul Comes Under Fire for Allegedly Hijacking Teen Anti-Smoking Curriculum."

53. Quoted in Allison Aubrey, "Parents: Teens Are Still Vaping Despite Flavor Ban. Here's What They're Using," NPR, February 17, 2020. www.npr.org.

54. Mitch McConnell: Senate Majority Leader, "McConnell Introduces Legislation to Make 21 the New Minimum Age for Purchasing Tobacco Products," May 20, 2019. www.republican leader.senate.gov.

55. Nicole Gaudiano, "Principals Laud New Bill to Raise Smoking Age to 21 as Vaping Increases in Schools," Politico, May 23, 2019. www.politico.com.

56. Dahlia Bazzaz, "The Legal Age to Buy Tobacco Is Now 21. Here's What That Means in Washington State," Seattle Times, December 18, 2019. www.seattletimes.com.

57. Bazzaz, "The Legal Age to Buy Tobacco is Now 21."

58. Quoted in U.S. Food & Drug Administration, "FDA Launches Its First Youth E-Cigarette Prevention TV Ads, Plans New Educational Resources As Agency Approaches One-Year Anniversary of Public Education Campaign," July 22, 2019. www .fda.gov.

59. CBS News, "Juul CEO Tells Non-Smokers Not to Vape or Use His Company's Product," August 29, 2019. www.cbsnews .com.

60. Ana Ibarra, "Vapers Seek Relief from Nicotine Addiction in—Wait for It—Cigarettes," NBC News, September 15, 2019. www.nbcnews.com.

Chapter Five: Kicking the Habit

61. Quoted in Meghna Chakrabarti, Allison Pohle, and Alex Schroeder, "Just How Hard Is It to Quit Vaping?," WBUR, October 8, 2019. www.wbur.org.

62. Quoted in Chakrabarti, Pohle, and Schroeder, "Just How Hard Is It to Quit Vaping?"

63. Quoted in Elly Yu, "High School Vape Culture Can Be Almost As Hard to Shake As Addiction, Teens Say," NPR, October 14, 2019. www.npr.org.

64. Quoted in Ashley Carman, "People Are Throwing Their JUULs out the Window and Drenching Them in Water Just to Quit," The Verge, September 11, 2019. www.theverge.com.

65. Jamie Putnam, "My Juul Breakup: 8 Steps That Helped Me Finally Quit Vaping," Everyday Health, November 20, 2019. www.everydayhealth.com.

66. Sue McGreevey, "What Makes AA Work?," The Harvard Gazette, September 12, 2011. https://news.harvard.edu.

67. Quoted in Truth Initiative, "This Is Quitting." https://truthinitiative.org.

68. Quoted in Elizabeth Gulino, "Here's How to Finally Put Down Your Juul," Refinery29, January 30, 2020. www.refinery29.com.

69. Quoted in Julie Mazziotta, "From Hot Ice to Swimming Pools, Teens Are Coming Up with Creative Ways to Ditch Their Vapes," People, January 6, 2020. https://people.com.

70. Jamie Ducharme, "Social Media Helped Juul Dominate the Vaping Market. Now, Teens Are Using It to Help Each Other Quit," Time, January 21, 2020. https://time.com.

71. Quoted in Lena Sun, "Some Patients with Vaping-Related Lung Injuries Are Being Hospitalized a Second Time," Washington Post, October 11, 2019. www.washingtonpost.com.

72. Lisa Mulcahy, "Consider This Your PSA: You Can Quit Vaping—and Here Are 8 Ways to Put Down the Pen!" Parade, February 18, 2020. https://parade.com.

American Lung Association—www.lung.org

The American Lung Association is an organization that works to improve lung health and prevent lung disease. One of its strategic objectives is to create a tobacco-free future. Its website provides informative reports on the dangers of e-cigarettes and vaping, as well as tips for people who hope to quit.

Centers for Disease Control and Prevention (CDC)
www.cdc.gov

The CDC is the United States' health protection agency. It works to protect Americans from health and safety threats. Its website has basic information on the prevalence and dangers of vaping. There are also in-depth articles and congressional testimony transcripts on topics such as the medical response to lung illnesses caused by e-cigarettes.

National Institute on Drug Abuse (NIDA)
www.drugabuse.gov

The NIDA's mission is to advance science on the causes and consequences of drug use and addiction. It applies its findings to improve individual and public health. The NIDA's website features information on e-cigarettes' effects on the brain, the consequences of children's exposure to nicotine, and fact sheets about vaping and associated paraphernalia.

Parents Against Vaping E-Cigarettes (PAVe)
www.parentsagainstvaping.org

PAVe is a grassroots organization formed by three mothers in New York City as a response to the youth vaping epidemic. Its website contains news stories from around the country about the dangers of vaping, resources for quitting, and details about PAVe's advocacy in the political world.

Partnership for Drug-Free Kids—www.drugfree.org

Partnership for Drug-Free Kids is an organization that works to prevent substance use among children and provides help for teens and young adults who are struggling with substance addiction. Its website includes information on vaping paraphernalia, its prevalence and consequences, and how to contact members of Congress to advocate for policies that reverse the vaping epidemic.

The Real Cost
FDA Center for Tobacco Products
https://therealcost.betobaccofree.hhs.gov

The Real Cost is one of the FDA's information campaigns. Its mandate is to educate teens about the effects of cigarettes, smokeless tobacco, and e-cigarettes. The website has "Real Facts" about vaping, including information on nicotine's effect on the brain and popcorn lung. There are also resources about how to quit using e-cigarettes.

Truth Initiative—www.truthinitiative.org

Truth Initiative is a nonprofit public health organization committed to ending tobacco use—particularly among children, teens, and young adults. Its website offers fact sheets on vaping statistics and vaping regulations, as well as many articles on the dangers and addictive qualities of e-cigarettes.

Books

John Allen. *Teens and Vaping*. San Diego, CA: ReferencePoint Press, 2020.

Kari Cornell, *E-Cigarettes and Their Dangers*. San Diego: Bright-Point, 2020.

Stephanie Lundquist-Arora. *Addiction: A Problem of Epidemic Proportions*. San Diego, CA: ReferencePoint Press, 2021.

Sherri Mabry Gordon, *Everything You Need to Know About Smoking, Vaping, and Your Health*. New York: Rosen, 2019.

Carla Mooney, *Addicted to E-Cigarettes and Vaping*. San Diego, CA: ReferencePoint Press, 2020.

Internet Sources

CDC, "Quick Facts on the Risks of E-Cigarettes for Kids, Teens, and Young Adults," February 3, 2020. www.cdc.gov.

Julie Creswell and Sheila Kaplan, "How Juul Hooked a Generation on Nicotine," *New York Times*, November 23, 2019. www.nytimes.com.

Jamie Ducharme, "How Juul Hooked Kids and Ignited a Public Health Crisis," *Time*, September 29, 2019. https://time.com.

Shira Feder, "A Teen Had a Double Lung Transplant Due to Vaping-Related Lung Damage," Insider, February 5, 2020. www.insider.com.

Angelica LaVito, "Trump Administration Readies Ban on Flavored E-Cigarettes amid Outbreak of Vaping Related Deaths," CNBC, September 11, 2019. www.cnbc.com.

Kari Paul, "Breaking Up with My Juul: Why Quitting Vaping Is Harder than Quitting Cigarettes," *The Guardian*, October 10, 2019. www.theguardian.com.

Kathleen Raven, "Nicotine Addiction from Vaping Is a Bigger Problem Than Teens Realize," Yale Medicine, March 19, 2019. www.yalemedicine.org.

Robert Shmerling, "Can Vaping Damage Your Lungs? What We Do (and Don't) Know," Harvard Health Publishing, September 4, 2019. www.health.harvard.edu.

Brendon Stiles and Steve Alperin, "We Ignored the Evidence Linking Cigarettes to Cancer. Let's Not Do That with Vaping," *The Guardian*, February 16, 2019. www.theguardian.com.

INDEX

Stephanie Lundquist-Arora has master's degrees in political science and public administration. She has written several books for teens and children, including *Addiction: A Problem of Epidemic Proportions*. When not writing, Lundquist-Arora likes traveling with her family, jogging, learning jiu-jitsu, reading, and trying new foods.